Old MacDonald's Barnyard Tales

DP

DEMPSEY
PARR

This is a Dempsey Parr Book, first published in 2000
Dempsey Parr is an imprint of Parragon
PARRAGON, Queen Street House, 4 Queen Street, Bath BA1 1HE, UK

Copyright © PARRAGON 2000

Created and produced by THE COMPLETE WORKS,
St. Mary's Road, Royal Leamington Spa, Warwickshire CV31 1JP, UK

Editorial Director: Mike Phipps
Project Manager: Stuart Branch
Editors: Aneurin Rhys & Julia Phipps
Designer: Gavin Scott

The Complete Works would like to thank Ellie for all of her help.

All rights reserved.
No part of this publication may be reproduced, stored in a retrieval system, or
transmitted by any means, electronic, mechanical, photocopying, recording or
otherwise, without the prior permission of the copyright holder.

ISBN 1-84084-872-3

Printed in Indonesia

Old MacDonald's
Barnyard
Tales

Written by Nicola Baxter
Illustrated by Caroline Davis

DP
DEMPSEY
PARR

contents

Old MacDonald had a farm, and on that farm he had some COWS...

Every day, my cows, Poppy, Annabel, Emily and Heather, moo and mumble, mumble and moo. I can't imagine what they talk about! But if you read on, you might just find out.

The new arrival

All day long, Old MacDonald's cows grazed in the green meadow. As they munched, they talked. Nothing much happened on the farm that Poppy, Annabel, Emily and Heather didn't know about.

One morning, Poppy was munching near the hedge, when Old MacDonald came to visit the horses in the field next door.

"Here's an apple for you, Tilly," he said, "and one for you, George. I want you to be the first to hear – we're expecting a new baby on the farm. You can imagine how excited Mrs. MacDonald is about it because..."

But before he could finish, there came the sound of thundering hooves, as a cow, bursting with news, dashed off to find her friends.

"Are you sure?" mooed Annabel, as Poppy panted out what she had heard.

"I'm sure." Poppy gasped.

"Old MacDonald and Mrs. MacDonald, aren't they, well, a bit old to have a baby?" asked Emily.

"I thought so," said Poppy. "But I heard it from Old MacDonald himself."

"But if Mrs. MacDonald has a baby to take care of," said Heather, "who will give me my beauty treatments before the County Show? I must win a rosette again this year."

There was complete silence. Then Annabel said what they had all been thinking.

"Ladies! This news is too important to keep to ourselves! We must tell the others immediately!" And off the four cows dashed.

So Emily leaned over the gate and mumbled in Jenny the hen's ear. "*What?*" she squawked. "If Mrs. MacDonald has a baby to take care of, who will collect my eggs? I must tell Henry!"

Henry the rooster crowed when he heard the news. "*Well, cock-a-doodle-doo!*" he cried. "If Mrs. MacDonald has a baby to take care of, who will throw me my corn to peck?" So Henry hurried off to talk to Debbie the duck.

And so it went on. Debbie told Milly the cat. Milly told Percy the pig. Percy told Bruce the sheepdog. And Bruce scampered off to tell Maria and the rest of the sheep.

13

14

By lunch time, every animal on the farm was worried. Things just wouldn't be the same if Mrs. MacDonald was taking care of a baby. The animals were so busy and bothered, they didn't notice a truck pulling into the barnyard.

"The new arrival!" called Old MacDonald.

"What, already?" squawked Jenny. "But I thought... oh!"

Out of the truck trotted a beautiful little foal – a new friend for Tilly and Old George.

"It's so good to have another baby animal on the farm!" cried Mrs. MacDonald.

She was too excited to hear the sigh of relief from all the animals, or the mooing from the meadow, as the other cows scolded Poppy!

Moo! Moo! Moo!

The Meadow Ladies Chorus,
Is something very new.
You'll hear them all clearly,
They're singing *"Moo! Moo! Moo!"*

They try to trill like parakeets,
And copy blackbirds, too.
The only song they really know,
Of course, is *"Moo! Moo! Moo!"*

They practise in the morning,
And in the nighttime, too.
It doesn't make a difference though,
They still sing *"Moo! Moo! Moo!"*

In Old MacDonald's barnyard,
You'll hear pigs oinking, too.
But louder still the ladies sing,
"Moo, Moo! Moo, Moo! Moo, Moo!"

17

A hat like that!

Heather the cow took great care of her appearance. No cow on the farm had such shiny hooves or such a glossy coat. She had already won three rosettes at the County Show, and she wanted to win more.

One windy afternoon, Heather was sheltering near a hedge. You can imagine her surprise when she found a beautiful straw hat on a branch. It had a couple of holes in it, but an elegant cow has to put her ears somewhere!

She strolled back across the field with her nose in the air, and the hat placed firmly on her head. Heather couldn't wait to show it off to her friends.

But Poppy, Annabel and Emily simply carried on munching. Heather tried a tiny lady-like cough. The munching didn't stop for a second. So Heather coughed a little louder. The munching grew louder.

Finally, Heather couldn't stand it any longer. "Haven't you noticed?" she mooed.

"Did someone say something?" asked Emily.

"It was me!" cried Heather, tossing her head.

"Oh," said Annabel, returning to a particularly juicy clump of green grass.

"I feel sleepy, I think I'll take a nap," said Poppy.

"And I'm going for a walk," said Emily.

Heather was not a patient cow. "Look at my hat!"

Of course, the other cows had noticed the hat, but they loved to tease their friend.

"I always think," said Poppy, "that hats are very – old-fashioned."

"Nonsense," Heather replied. "Only the most fashionable cows are wearing them."

"Is it new then?" asked Annabel.

"Certainly!" Heather replied. "It's the latest style."

"Didn't Mrs. MacDonald have a hat like that a few years ago?" asked Emily.

"I don't think so!" Heather said firmly. "Mrs. MacDonald is a delight, but she's not stylish. Only a prize-winning cow could wear a hat like this."

"If you say so, dear," mooed Annabel.

23

That evening, the cows ambled into the barnyard as usual to be milked. Before long, all the other animals gathered round.

"They're admiring my hat!" whispered Heather to Poppy.

But the giggling and chuckling didn't sound like animals who thought Heather looked beautiful. It sounded like animals who thought she looked silly.

"So that's what happened to Scarecrow Sam's hat!"

cried Old MacDonald.

These days, when Heather starts putting on airs and graces, Poppy, Emily and Annabel know what to do – talk turns from ears and horns to hats, and Heather tiptoes away.

You need a cow!

How does fresh milk reach your shake,
The frothy, creamy kind you make?
You ask how?
You need a cow!

How does butter reach your bread,
The slithery, slippery stuff you spread?
You ask how?
You need a cow!

How does your cheese reach your plate,
The yummy, yellow kind you grate?
You ask how?
You need a cow!

How does ice cream reach your spoon,
The kind you cannot eat too soon?
You ask how?
You need a cow!

27

Nibbling neighbours

One sunny morning in the meadow, Annabel was happily munching grass when she was surprised to discover a hole where there should be grass. "My dears," she mooed, "there's a hole in our field!"

There was no doubt about it. Someone had dug a large, round, deep hole in the ground.

"We must be careful not to fall into it," said Poppy, anxiously.

But the next morning, where there was one hole, now there were five! "If this goes on," said Poppy, "we'll have nowhere to stand at all!"

"And nothing to eat," added Emily in alarm.

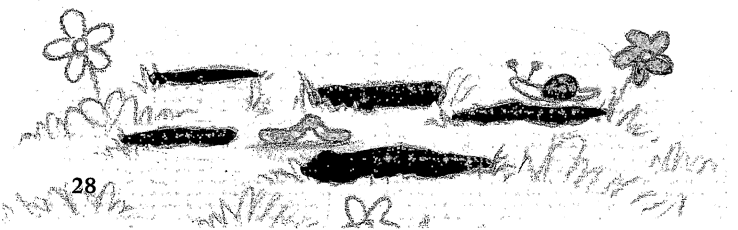

By the end of the week, there were over a hundred holes dotted around the meadow.

"You've got some nibbling neighbours," said Old MacDonald. "It looks like a family of rabbits has come to stay."

The cows shuddered. "Those little hopping things with long ears?" said Heather. "How can I look my best with them around?"

"And they have very, very large families," warned Emily. "Not just one baby at a time, like cows do."

"It's strange we've never seen one," said Poppy thoughtfully. "Maybe they do their digging in the dark. I'm going to keep watch tonight."

So, that night, as the full moon rose over the meadow, Poppy pretended to sleep.

And although she was expecting it, she was still shocked when two bright little eyes and a twitchy nose popped up right in front of her.

"Aaaaaghh!"

cried Poppy.

"Aaaaaghh!"

cried the rabbit, as it disappeared down its hole faster than ever.

"You should follow it!" said Annabel, who was awakened by the noise.

"Down a rabbit hole?" gasped Emily. "Don't be silly, Annabel. She's too big!"

"Then we're doomed," said Heather, gloomily. "Those rabbits will take over without us seeing them do it."

The next morning, the cows awakened to an amazing sight. Hundreds of rabbits were sitting all around them.

"Excuse me!" said the largest one. "We have come to ask for your help."

"Help?" echoed Annabel. "We're the ones who need help!"

The rabbit said that his family lived in fear. "Your hooves are so big," he explained, "you could stamp on us without noticing."

Just then, Poppy had one of her excellent ideas. "You would be safer," she said, "if you lived under the hedge."

It worked perfectly. All day in the meadow, there is munching, mooing and mumbling. All night in the hedge, there is nibbling, digging and wiggling. And *everyone* is happy.

Old MacDonald had a farm,

E-I-E-I-O!
And on that farm he had some cows,
E-I-E-I-O!
With a moo, moo here
And a moo, moo there.
Here a moo,
There a moo,
Everywhere a moo, moo!
Old MacDonald had a farm,
E-I-E-I-O!

Old MacDonald had a farm, and on that farm he had some SHEEP...

I love all the animals on my farm,
but the woolly ones really keep me on my toes!
They love to leap so much, sometimes they jump
right out of the farm and set off over the hills.
Then I have to look for them.
I always find them in the end and bring
them home. Then they look a bit
—*sheepish*!

Maria's haircut

One spring day, Maria the sheep stood by the pond in Old MacDonald's barnyard, gazing sadly into the water.

"What is she doing?" whispered Doris the duck to her friend Dora. "It's unusual to see sheep near water."

Meanwhile, lots of little ducklings swam across to see who the visitor was.

"Sheep don't eat ducklings, do they?" asked Dora, anxiously. She was not a smart duck!

"Of course not!" replied Doris. "Our ducklings are quite safe with Maria."

But just then, Maria gave *such* a big sigh that all the ducklings blew right across the pond and had to be rescued by their mothers!

Old George the horse couldn't stand to see another animal on the farm unhappy. He clip-clopped across the yard and gently rubbed his big head against Maria's woolly back. "What's the trouble, my dear?" he asked. "Has your lamb run away again?"

"No." Maria sighed. "It isn't that. Look at me!"

Old George looked carefully at Maria. "Well, you look even more, er, wonderfully woolly than usual," he said, gallantly.

"I look terrible," said Maria. "My coat should have been trimmed weeks ago, but Old MacDonald has forgotten."

"Hmmmm. He can be forgetful," said Old George. "I'll talk to the other animals and see what they suggest."

The animals were most interested in Maria's problem. "Perhaps I could nibble her coat," suggested Percy the pig, who ate almost anything! But no-one liked this idea.

"No, we need to remind Old MacDonald to give Maria a haircut," said Poppy the cow. "But how do we do it?"

"Old MacDonald is always so busy," added Henrietta the hen. "I don't think he would notice what we did!"

And that gave Poppy a good idea. "No," she mooed, "when it comes to noticing things, it's Mrs. MacDonald we need. Perhaps you should do some nibbling after all, Percy."

So, Percy did a little nibbling, and the hens scurried away with the tufts of wool in their beaks, and determined looks on their faces, searching for the farmer.

When Old MacDonald went in for his lunch that day, Mrs. MacDonald threw her hands up in horror!

"MacD!" she cried. "You're covered in wool! Don't you dare bring all that fluffy stuff into my clean kitchen! It's time those sheep were shorn."

The very next day, Maria's haircut was the talk of the barnyard. And she and her friends strutted happily around, looking as smart and as stylish as any sheep you've ever seen.

Woolly coats

In the middle of the winter,
All the animals complain,
"Our furry coats are much too thin.
They let the icy north wind in.
We want to go inside again!"

But while the rest shiver,
Sheep are fine and look quite smug,
"We will not come to any harm.
We're the warmest on the farm.
Our woolly coats will keep us
snug!"

48

In the middle of the summer,
Animals laze in the sun and smile.
"How we love this sunny weather.
We sit outside and talk together.
Can it be summer all the while?"

But as the beasts all talk,
Sheep grumble under trees.
"Even when our coats are shorn,
We still are much too warm.
We cannot wait for it to
freeze!"

49

Snowy and blowy

Old MacDonald peeked out of his window one day and decided to put on three extra sweaters.

"That's very sensible," said Mrs. MacDonald. "You need to keep warm when it's snowy."

"What worries me," said Old MacDonald, "is that it's snowy *and* blowy. I must make sure that the sheep are safe. It's time they came down from the meadow."

Old MacDonald puffed and panted as he put on his boots and set off for the meadow, taking Bruce the sheepdog with him.

But the sheep were nowhere to be seen. They were completely hidden by the snow!

"It's days like these," said Old MacDonald, "that I wish I had black sheep instead of white ones."

Suddenly, Bruce started to behave in a strange way, jumping up and down with his paws together, just like sheep do!

But Old MacDonald understood. He laughed and patted Bruce's head. Then he cupped his hands around his mouth and shouted, "Today there will be a jumping competition! It will keep us warm. I think the rabbits in the next field will win!"

Woosh! One energetic sheep jumped up, showering snow all around. Woosh! Woosh! Two more leapt into the air, shaking the snow from their coats. Suddenly, the field was full of leaping, jumping sheep!

Those sheep made quite sure that the rabbits in the next field didn't stand a chance. But, those rabbits were all snugly asleep in their burrows, unaware what anybody thought of their jumping.

Back in the barnyard, the other animals soon saw how warm and happy the woolly jumpers were. And before long, everyone was at it!

Except Old MacDonald, who puffed and panted and tried to get his boots off, and Bruce, who was too busy with his dinner to think of anything else!

Counting sheep

Old MacDonald's counting sheep,
It's not because he cannot sleep.
He's wondering if maybe,
Each sheep has had her baby.

"Stand still!" he cries. *"Keep still and steady*
I might have counted you already!"
But little lambs can't stop dancing,
And even sheep love lots of prancing.

The counting keeps the farmer busy,
Poor Old MacDonald's feeling dizzy!
Then suddenly he starts to smile.
"Goodbye! I'll see you in a while."

When all the farm is soundly sleeping,
Old MacDonald's softly creeping.
It's really easy to count sheep,
When you're awake and they're asleep!

Lost for ever

Sheep are fine animals, but they are not the smartest creatures on the farm. They follow one another without thinking whether it is a good idea. When the leader is Maria, it isn't!

One day, Maria thought that the grass in the next meadow was much greener and juicier than the grass right under her nose.

"Come on, girls!" she baa-ed. "Follow me!"

With a skip and a jump, Maria was over the fence and into the meadow next door.

It wasn't long before the other sheep had followed Maria into the next field, too.

After an hour or so of munching grass in the new meadow, Maria looked over the wall on the far side. The grass there looked even better. "Follow me!" she baa-ed again, and she was off! The other sheep were right behind her.

By the end of the afternoon, Maria and her friends found themselves a long way from Old MacDonald's farm and were likely to be lost for ever!

"I don't know where we are," said Maria, looking all around her. "Oh, I won't worry now. I'm going to sleep."

And, of course, all the other sheep were soon asleep, too.

OLD MACDONALD'S FARM THIS WAY ➡

When sheep wake up, they are hungry! So next morning, when Maria awoke, she forgot all about finding her way home. Instead, she tucked into some yummy grass.

You can guess what the other sheep did!

Maria grazed her way across the meadow and came to a hedge. Over the hedge was another meadow, and the grass looked even more yummy there. "Follow me, girls!" Maria baa-ed. So, with a skip and a jump, the flock leaped into the meadow and started on their mid-morning snack.

At lunch time, dinner time and supper time, exactly the same thing happened.

It wasn't until bed time that Maria remembered they were a long way from home. "We must be even further now," she baa-ed, sadly.

"But maaamaaa…"

bleated her little lamb.

"Tell me in the morning," Maria replied.

"But maaamaaa…"

the lamb tried again.

"Go to sleep, little one," said Maria. "We'll get home tomorrow."

"But MAAAMAAA!" laughed the little lamb. "We are home already. Look!"

And there was Old MacDonald's meadow. The smoke from the farmhouse chimney drifted into the evening air. Without meaning to, Maria had led them all the way back home again.

Although sheep are not smart creatures, sometimes they are silly in a very smart way (if you see what I mean)!

Old MacDonald had a farm

E-I-E-I-O!
And on that farm he had some sheep,
E-I-E-I-O!
With a baa, baa here
And a baa, baa there.
Here a baa,
There a baa,
Everywhere a baa, baa!
Old MacDonald had a farm,
E-I-E-I-O!

Old MacDonald had a farm, and on that farm he had some HORSES...

Woah! Steady there, George! You'll get your dinner in a second. Let me just check your shoes first. You and Tilly are the biggest animals on the farm, but you're a lot less trouble than others! I want to tell everyone what good friends you've been to me.

The good old days

On cold, wet and windy afternoons, when Old MacDonald lets his animals shelter in the warm barn, there is nothing they like better than listening to stories. But, it does depend on who's telling the story!

The pigs always tell tales about food. The hens' stories are usually about the ducks, and the cows are terrible gossips – they repeat things they have half-heard!

But Old George and Tilly, the oldest animals on the farm, always talk about days gone by and how much better it was then. The other animals are bored with these stories. They have heard them many times before.

One very cold Spring day, when the farm was full of newborn chicks, Old MacDonald went to the hen house and said to Henrietta, "Take your babies into the barn. The rest of the animals are in there already. It will be much cosier there than in here."

"Baaa!" bleated Maria the sheep, who was standing near the barn door. "Did you hear that? Henrietta is bringing her chicks in. There'll be no peace now!"

Suddenly, there was mooing, neighing, snorting and quacking as the other animals agreed. Those tiny chicks were the most troublesome little creatures on the farm. And the animals all stared in dismay as, one by one, the chicks filed in.

That afternoon, it was Percy the pig's turn to tell a story. **"Once upon a time,"** he began, **"there lived a pig who was very hungry..."**

But although the animals tried to concentrate, the lively little chicks made it very difficult to listen. They pecked at Heather the cow's nose and made her sneeze. They scratched at Bruce the sheepdog's tail until he was forced to bark quite sharply at them. One of them even tried to go to sleep in Maria the sheep's woolly ear. It was very distracting and it made all the animals grouchy.

"... something very, very delicious. The end," said Percy, only too aware that no-one had been able to listen to his story. He oinked loudly at the chicks and stomped off into a corner to sulk.

75

Next, it was Old George the horse's turn. **"My tale,"** he said, **"is about the good old days…"**

All the animals, except Tilly, groaned. Of course, they did it very quietly so that they wouldn't upset Old George. But a boring story and a barn full of mischievous chicks was a recipe for a boring afternoon.

But, as Old George droned on and on and on, an amazing thing happened. Every one of the chirping chicks began to fall asleep in the warmth of Henrietta's feathers.

"… and that reminds me of another story," said Old George, **"but I don't imagine you want to hear that today."**

"Oh, yes! Yes, we do!" said the other animals. "We love your stories, George!" And they meant every word of it!

Clip, clop!

Pigs can prance,
And ducks can dance,
Hens flutter in a flurry.
But George plods on and doesn't stop,
Clip, clop! Clip, clop!
He's *never* in a hurry.

Lambs can leap,
And cats can creep,
Cows kick their heels and scurry.
But George plods on and doesn't stop,
Clip, clop! Clip, clop!
He's *never* in a hurry.

"Of course, I know
My horse is slow,
But I will never worry.
For George plods on and doesn't stop,
Clip, clop! Clip, clop!
He doesn't *need* to hurry."

Horse power

On the day of the County Show, there was a hustling and a bustling on the farm. Mrs. MacDonald had to feed the animals and collect the eggs by herself, as Old MacDonald was busy cleaning his tractor.

Every year, Old MacDonald drove his tractor and trailer to the show to give rides to the children. They loved it, but it meant a lot of hard work for the farmer. There were wheels to wash, and the hood to polish. And today, there were even ducks to shoo away when they began splashing about in the bubbles in his pail!

Finally, the tractor was spotlessly clean. Old MacDonald went into the farmhouse to put on his best boots.

"Here we go," said Doris the duck, as the farmer climbed into his tractor. "Cover your ears, little ones!"

But when Old MacDonald turned the key, there was silence. The tractor simply would not start.

Old MacDonald fiddled with the engine — and got his hands dirty. He stamped and stomped around — and got his very best boots muddy. He muttered and grumbled — and got red in the face. None of it helped. The tractor didn't cough or splutter or show any sign of life.

"I hate to let all of the children down." Old MacDonald groaned. "But I can't pull the trailer if I don't have a tractor."

Now, Henry the rooster is often mischievous and always nosy, but sometimes he has good ideas. As Old George and Tilly looked out into the yard, Henry jumped up onto their stable door and gave his loudest,

"Cock-a-doodle-doo!"

Old MacDonald looked up in surprise and delight.

"Goodness, gracious me!" he cried. "You're right, Henry – horse power! Now quick, jump out of the way. There's lots of work to be done!"

There were coats to comb, tails to untangle and manes to thread with pretty ribbons. There were harnesses to hitch and reins to clean and hang with gleaming brasses.

"It's just like the good old days," neighed Old George to Tilly.

There was no doubt who the stars of the County Show were that year. Children stood in a long line waiting to be pulled around the show ground by Old George and Tilly. The horses plodded proudly up and down with their coats shining and their heads held high.

At the end of the afternoon, Old MacDonald led the horses back to their stable and gave them a special supper of apples and oats.

"You know," he said, as he stroked their manes, "sometimes I miss the old days, too."

But when Old George and Tilly nodded their big heads, it wasn't to show they agreed. They were fast asleep on their feet. After all, they're not so young anymore, and it had been a busy day!

A horse, of course!

Who can you trust when the
tractor breaks down,
And the nearest mechanic is off
in the town?
Who is as big and as strong as a horse?
Oh, silly me, a horse, of course!

Who do you know who can eat
tons of hay,
And even munch ten sacks of
oats in a day?
Who has an appetite as large as a horse?
Oh, silly me, a horse, of course!

Who will stick by you when you
need a friend,
And hear all your troubles right through
to the end?
Who is as wise and as kind as a horse?
Oh, silly me, a horse, of course!

89

A good example

Tilly and Old George were friendly old horses, but they didn't really understand the young animals who tore around the barnyard.

"Look at that piglet," Tilly grumbled. "He's leaving muddy trotter-prints all over the yard."

"And those noisy chicks and ducklings are not behaving well." Old George nodded his head in agreement. "They should never cheep and quack during our afternoon nap."

"Things were different in the old days," sighed Tilly. "Youngsters were raised properly then. When we were foals, we were tidy and very, very quiet."

Unfortunately, Tilly and Old George didn't keep their feelings to themselves...

Next morning, Tilly told Percy the pig how he should discipline his piglets. Old George gave Jenny and Henrietta the hens useful tips on raising chicks. And both the horses had a word with Doris the duck about the right time and place for ducklings to quack.

By lunch time, there wasn't a single animal on the barnyard who wasn't feeling angry with Tilly and Old George.

"I'd like to see them taking care of even one little one," said Doris.

Strangely enough, it was that afternoon Old MacDonald brought a new foal to the farm for Tilly and Old George to care for. Percy, Jenny, Henrietta and Doris looked forward to having some fun!

But the animals were very disappointed. The new foal, whose name was Frances, was so good. She never spilled her oats, or splashed the water in her trough. She wasn't noisy, or nosy, or mischievous.

Worse, Tilly and Old George looked so pleased with themselves.

"You see," Old George told Percy, "it's just a matter of setting a good example. When a young animal sees her parents being quiet and sensible, she copies them."

As Percy snorted with disgust, Old George made a big, sweeping gesture with his hoof, and his shoe, which was loose, flew right off!

The shoe shot across the barnyard.
Clang! It knocked over a pail of
pig food. Clonk! It bounced off the pail
and whizzed straight through a window
and into the farmhouse. Crash!

Mrs. MacDonald stormed out into the
yard. She was holding an apple pie with a
large horseshoe sticking in it!

"Who has done this?" She cried.
"And made so much noise and mess?"

Old George tried very, very hard to look
unconcerned, but the eyes of every other
animal in the barnyard were upon him.
Who else had shoes that big?

These days, Tilly and Old George are not
so quick to criticize their friends. And the
story of George's flying footwear still brings
a smile to everyone's face, (all except for
Mrs. MacDonald, of course)!

Old MacDonald had a farm,

E-I-E-I-O!
And on that farm he had some horses,
E-I-E-I-O!
With a neigh, neigh here
And a neigh, neigh there
Here a neigh,
There a neigh,
Everywhere a neigh, neigh!
Old MacDonald had a farm,
E-I-E-I-O!

Come on, ladies!
Plenty of corn for you today.
Don't squabble, Jenny! Henrietta
needs her breakfast, too. And you
needn't cock-a-doodle-doo at me,
Henry! I haven't forgotten you.
What's that you're saying?
There's trouble with the hen
house? Tell me more.

Old MacDonald had a farm, and on that farm he had some HENS...

Home, sweet home

Old MacDonald always worked hard, but these days he was extra busy in his workshop. One bright, sunny morning, he was finally ready to show everyone what he had been making. "Here you are, ladies!" he cried. "A new hen house for you – and Henry the rooster, of course. I don't like to think of you shivering in your home. The wind whistles through those cracks, doesn't it?"

Jenny and the rest of the hens hurried over, clucking with curiosity. Henry flapped up on to the roof to see if it was a comfortable place for crowing. "Cock-a-doodle-not-bad-at-all," he crowed, as Jenny, Henrietta, Mary and Victoria hopped into their new home.

For two days, the hens were very happy inside the new hen house. But, the ducks, being that little bit jealous, squawked and squabbled more than usual and started to sulk a lot.

On the third day, Jenny the hen finally said what the other hens were thinking. "You know, there was something to be said for the cracks in our old home," she clucked. "We could even keep an eye on those silly ducks without ever going outside." Henry crowed his agreement!

"You're right," agreed Henrietta. "And our old perches were more comfortable, too."

"And," clucked Mary, "this place smells very funny! I suppose it's the paint, but I'm not sure I want to raise chicks here."

It wasn't long before the hens and Henry decided that they wanted to move back to their old home.

"I could cock-a-doodle-doo right over the pig sty from there," said Henry. "I used to like talking with Percy first thing in the morning."

That evening, when Mrs. MacDonald came out to feed the hens, Old MacDonald came, too. "Doesn't that look better?" he said, proudly patting the hen house roof.

"It's a bit near the flower garden for me," said his wife, looking at Henry, who liked eating her marigolds!

The hens knew how proud Old MacDonald was of the new hen house. They couldn't bear to hurt his feelings by returning to their old home. They would just have to be happy with this one.

A few days later, it was Milly the cat – who wasn't the best of friends with the feathered folk of the farm – who solved the problem.

While the hens and Henry were scratching around in the barn, Milly crept into the brand new hen house. It was exactly the cosy place she was looking for. "This is purr-fect," she said.

Later that day, Old MacDonald had a quiet word with Henry and the hens. "I'm sorry," he said, "but Milly has just had her kittens in your new home. We won't be able to disturb her for a few weeks. Could you…"

And before he could finish, the hens and Henry were scuttling through the door of their dear old home. "Home, sweet home," the hens clucked. (It's amazing how helpful hens can be sometimes!)

Egg-hatching dream

When Jenny is sitting,
And sitting, and sitting,
She can't do any knitting,
Or sew a fine seam.

If her eggs are to hatch,
Every one of the batch,
There is nothing to match,
An egg-hatching dream.

She dreams of bananas,
Of pears and piranhas,
Of soap and sultanas,
And other strange things.

She thinks about field mice,
And carpets and creamy rice,
And whether bees taste nice,
For mid-morning snacks.

Her thoughts travel far and near.
Half asleep she'll appear,
Until she starts to hear,
Her eggs start to crack!

110

111

The fluffy chicks

Most of the time, the hens and ducks on the farm are friendly, but every now and then they have a disagreement and, for a few days, the barnyard is not a peaceful place! The funniest fight between the hens and ducks began when Doris the duck came to see Jenny the hen...

"I know how boring it can be waiting for eggs to hatch," began Doris. "So I thought you might like a visitor. Well, you will never guess what I... "

In fact, Jenny was dreaming a pleasant dream about wiggly worms, but she opened her eyes and tried to be as polite as possible while she listened.

Ten minutes later, both Doris and Jenny heard a teeney-weeney tap-tapping sound...

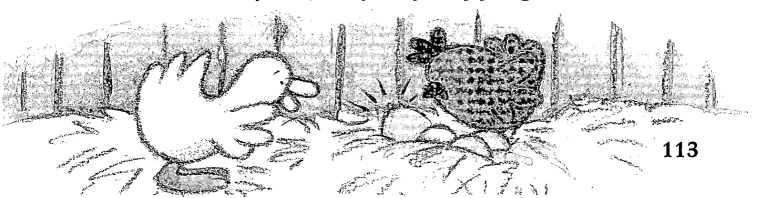

Suddenly, seven fluffy chicks tap-tapped their way out of their eggs and poked through Jenny's feathers to take their first look at the world.

But the first thing they saw was not Jenny, their mom, but the tiny, bright eyes of Doris!

And that is why, when Doris rushed out of the hen house, desperate to pass on the news to her friends on the duck pond, seven little chicks followed her right out of the door!

"Come back!" clucked Jenny. But it was too late. One duck and seven tiny little chicks were waddling across the barnyard, heading for Doris's nest in the reeds around the pond.

"Stop!" cried Jenny. "What do you think you're doing, Doris?"

When Doris saw what was happening, she couldn't help smiling. "They like me, Jenny dear," she said. "There's nothing I can do about it."

But it wasn't long before Doris became tired of being followed everywhere. She wanted to swim, but she was afraid the fluffy chicks might jump in as well!

"Call them home, Jenny!" she shouted to the hen, who was dozing in the sunshine.

But Jenny knew that Doris was taking good care of her babies. "They seem to like you, Doris dear," she said. "There's nothing I can do about it!"

For two long days, the chicks thought they were ducklings. When they opened their little beaks, they quacked just like Doris!

Then, on the second evening, it began to rain. *Splish*! *Splash*! *Splosh*! Heavy, wet drops fell on the ground. *Splish*! *Splash*! In no time at all, the barnyard was covered in puddles.

"Hooray!" shouted Doris and all the other ducks. They stamped and splashed, quacked and laughed.

"Ugh!" squawked the seven little chicks, and they scurried back to the hen house as fast as their little legs would carry them. They didn't like getting wet at all!

The chicks settled happily under Jenny's warm feathers. They were happy not to be ducks after all! And these days, Doris is careful before she disturbs Jenny – especially when she's sitting on her eggs!

119

One hen pecking

One hen pecking in the garden –
Mrs. MacDonald shakes
her head.

Two hens pecking in the garden –
Makes her shake her
fist instead!

Three hens pecking in the garden
The farmer's wife comes
storming out.

Four hens pecking in the garden –
Mrs. MacDonald starts
to shout.

Henry the rooster in the garden –
Pecking all the while –
Brings a lovely bunch of flowers –
Mrs. MacDonald has
to smile.

Trampling trotters

Near the farmhouse, Mrs. MacDonald had a little garden. She was usually very busy on the farm, but somehow she always found time to look after the flowers she loved so much. Unfortunately, the hens also loved the flowers – for very different reasons!

"Marigolds are delicious," Henry would mutter, talking with his beak full as usual.

Mrs. MacDonald kept an eye on the hens through the kitchen window. If she saw them tip-toeing into the garden, she would rush out, waving a tea towel. "Shoo, you greedy birds!" she would call. "Leave my flowers alone!" And Henry and the hens would flutter away – for a while.

Early one morning, Old MacDonald and Mrs. MacDonald got ready to go to the local market. Mrs. MacDonald had one last word with the hens before they set off. "There is plenty of grain for you in the hen house," she said. "There is no need for you to go into my garden. Do you understand?"

The hens eagerly nodded and clucked, but whether this meant that they agreed or not, Mrs. MacDonald wasn't quite sure.

As Old MacDonald's van disappeared down the lane, Henry the rooster strutted towards an especially beautiful clump of marigolds.

Jenny the hen scuttled anxiously after him. "Henry," she warned, "if we peck at those flowers, Mrs. MacDonald is going to be angry. Remember what happened last time!"

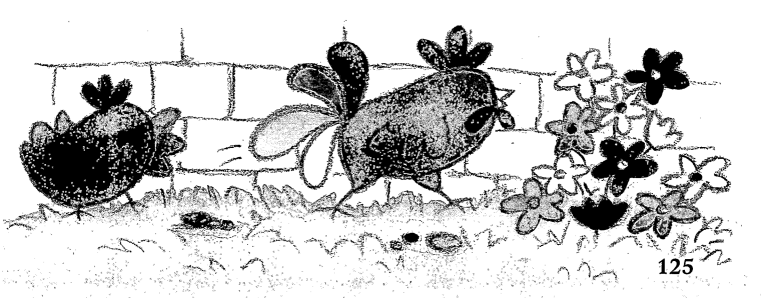

Henry was just thinking about those awful scenes when something large and pink rushed past him.

It was Percy the pig!

In his hurry that lovely sunny morning, Old MacDonald had left the gate of the pig sty slightly open. Percy loved to run around the barnyard. Today he was heading straight for Mrs. MacDonald's garden.

That bad pig rolled over and over on the flower beds. He rooted under the begonias. He jumped onto the marigolds. By the time he had finished and was trotting happily on his way, the garden was in an awful mess.

"Are you thinking what I'm thinking?" asked Henry.

"Yes," gulped the hens. "She'll think it was us!"

Now, hens are not known for hard work, but that morning, Jenny, Henrietta, Mary, Victoria and Henry worked *very* hard indeed.

They stood up sagging flowers. Stamped down the uprooted earth. They tried very hard to clear up the dirt made by Percy's trampling trotters.

But when they heard Old MacDonald's van coming down the lane, the garden still looked a sight.

The hens and Henry lined up beside the garden. They wanted to know the worst straightaway. There was a long silence as Mrs. MacDonald surveyed the scene.

Finally, she said, "Don't worry, ladies. Don't worry, Henry. I can see that someone bigger and bulkier than you has been bouncing in my begonias. We'll all have a special snack before I deal with that pig!"

129

Old MacDonald had a farm,
E-I-E-I-O!
And on that farm he had some hens,
E-I-E-I-O!
With a cluck, cluck here
And a cluck, cluck there.
Here a cluck,
There a cluck,
Everywhere a cluck, cluck!
Old MacDonald had a farm,
E-I-E-I-O!

131

Old MacDonald had a farm, and on that farm he had a TRACTOR...

Hello there! I'm Old MacDonald. Taking care of my animals keeps me busy, I can tell you. I never know what they'll get up to next. But I have crops to plant and take care of, too. I couldn't manage all the work without my tractor – even if it is just as much trouble as the animals sometimes!

So many colors!

Old MacDonald looked out over his field of yellow corn with pride.

"Another couple of days and it will be ready for cutting," he said to Mrs. MacDonald. "I've never seen such a fine crop."

"You can't say that for this gate," said his wife. "Look at the way the paint is peeling off! It's a disgrace."

"Then my first job today will be painting it," declared Old MacDonald. "Just leave it to me, my dear!" And he hurried off to the barnyard to find the old pots of paint and brushes he kept in the barn.

It wasn't long before Old MacDonald was back at the gate with lots of paint. A long line of curious animals had followed him to see what was going on.

"Give me some room, Jenny!" he told the hen, as she poked her beak into the first pot of paint he opened – it was a bright red color.

"That will do," said Old MacDonald. "There is plenty here to finish the job."

But Jenny couldn't resist taking another look into the paint pot while the farmer was busy painting. And when he turned back to dip his brush in again...

Squawk! The pot overturned, spilling the paint everywhere! Jenny was covered – and her little legs were not yellow any more but bright red!

"Well, never mind," said Old MacDonald, as Jenny hopped back to the barnyard. "I'll just open another pot. What about this one?"

The farmer was soon busy painting again, this time he was using a bright green. What a pity Annabel the cow chose that moment to come racing over to see what was happening. She did see Old MacDonald – but she didn't see the pot of paint. **Clang!** It went flying up into the air. **Clunk!** It landed over Percy the pig's head.

"**That's it!**" cried Old MacDonald. "I've had enough interruptions for today. Back to the barnyard everyone, and let me get on in peace."

Then Old MacDonald opened a pot of yellow paint and set to work. "This is much better," he said, as he stood back to admire his handiwork. "Now, how am I doing?"

The farmer took a step back and – whoops! One more pot was spilled, (and guess who now had very yellow boots)!

Ten minutes later, Old MacDonald was putting the finishing touches to the bottom rail, this time using blue paint!

It was then that Mrs. MacDonald came to see how he was getting on.

"Now, is that better?" said Old MacDonald.

Mrs. MacDonald blinked. She had never seen so many colors before! "I'll tell you as soon as I put my sunglasses on!" She laughed.

Busy farmer

When a very busy farmer,
Goes upstairs to bed at night,
He simply can't stop wondering,
If everything's all right.

Are the ducklings in the garden?
Are the piglets in the pond?
Are the sheep safe in the meadow,
Or roaming far beyond?

Are the cows asleep and dreaming?
Are they trotting down the lane?
Is the rooster in the kitchen,
Pecking at the pies again?

So a very busy farmer,
Always rises at first light.
He simply cannot wait to check,
That everything's all right.

143

Tractor trouble

Old MacDonald loves his tractor, but it can be as troublesome as a mischievious piglet sometimes. One cold and frosty morning, it sat in the barn and refused to start.

"I must plough the far field today," groaned Old MacDonald. "Before long, the new lambs will begin to be born. Then I'll have no time at all for ploughing."

But the tractor would not start! It coughed and wheezed a bit, and a few puffs of black smoke came out of the exhaust pipe. But there was none of the roaring and revving that Old MacDonald liked to hear.

"I'll just have to call the mechanic," he said crossly, stomping towards the farmhouse.

Unfortunately, the mechanic was busy for the rest of the week.

"Listen carefully, and I'll tell you what to look for," he told Old MacDonald helpfully.

So the farmer tramped back to the barn, his head full of thoughts of pipes, plugs and pumps. He wasn't at all sure he had understood a word the mechanic had said!

But the moment Old MacDonald opened up the engine's bonnet, he knew exactly what the problem was – and he wasn't angry at all. A little mouse had made her nest there and was busy taking care of six tiny babies!

"Don't worry," whispered Old MacDonald, "I'll find you somewhere better to live."

So Old MacDonald started searching the barn for a home for the mouse and her family. It had to be warm and cosy. It had to be somewhere that Milly and Lazy the cats couldn't reach. It had to be a very special place.

Looking through all the junk and clutter kept at the back of the barn was hot work. Old MacDonald took off his coat and hung it from a beam. By the end of the morning, the barn looked neater, but he still hadn't found a home for the mouse family.

"Come and have your lunch," called his wife. "And don't even think about bringing those mice into my kitchen!"

But, as Old MacDonald took his coat from the beam, he suddenly had an idea...

Ten minutes later, the mouse family had a good new home, and Old MacDonald was enjoying his lunch at last.

"I'm off to plough the fields now," he said to his wife when he had finished. "Where is my old jacket?"

Mrs. MacDonald looked surprised. "Why?" she began. Then she smiled. "I suppose you've lent your coat to someone else for a while."

Old MacDonald found his old coat and went back to the barn. This time there wasn't any tractor trouble – the machine roared into life.

"Less noise until we get outside, old friend," smiled Old MacDonald. "We don't want to wake the babies."

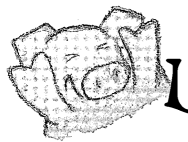

Loves to sing!

Old MacDonald loves to sing,
While doing all his chores.
His wife just thanks her lucky stars,
He does it out of doors!

It's like a lost lamb's bleat,
A hungry horse's neigh.
The kind of snort a piglet makes,
When rolling in the hay!

It's like a chicken's squawk,
A tiny baby's wail.
The sound a sleepy cat would make,
If you stepped on her tail!

So Old MacDonald's wife just cooks.
While her husband gets no thinner,
Because MacDonald cannot sing,
With his mouth full of dinner!

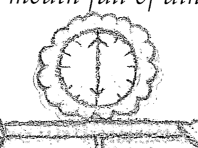

Good teamwork

It had been raining heavily for days and days on Old MacDonald's farm. Even the ducks started to wish the sun would come out.

"It's no good," said the farmer one morning at breakfast. "I will have to take the tractor down to the bottom meadow and see if the stream is overflowing. I can't have my sheep getting wet feet!"

Old MacDonald put on his raincoat and hat and set off on the tractor, but he didn't get very far. The gateway to the barnyard had become very muddy.

Brrrrm! Vrrrrm! Brrrrm!
The tractor did its best, but it was soon stuck in the mud!

The rain trickled off Old MacDonald's nose as he climbed down from his tractor. He shook his head when he saw the mud. "Only my old friend George can help me now," he said.

Old George the horse didn't want to go out in the rain, but he stood patiently as the farmer harnessed him to the tractor.

"Now pull, George, *PULL!*" he yelled. Old George pulled as hard as he could – the tractor wouldn't budge.

"I need two horses," said Old MacDonald, and he went to fetch Tilly.

Tilly and Old George pulled as hard as they could – the tractor wouldn't move. The ducks stood in a long line, watching with interest.

"If only I had another horse," said Old MacDonald. Suddenly, he had an idea. Before you could say, *"You must be joking!"* the farmer had brought out his four cows to help.

Old George, Tilly, Annabel, Poppy, Heather and Emily pulled and pulled and pulled – the tractor still wouldn't move.

Old MacDonald was getting desperate. One by one, he called on Percy the pig, Maria the sheep, Bruce the sheepdog and his two cats – even Mrs. MacDonald came to help.

The rain still poured down and down. The MacDonalds and their animals tugged and pulled. They pulled and they tugged. But the tractor stayed exactly where it was!

159

160

"I'll help!" Jenny the hen clucked, and she took a *very* firm hold of Milly the cat's tail in her beak.

Milly howled. Lazy yowled. Bruce yelped. Maria bleated. Percy oinked. The cows mooed and the horses neighed. Old MacDonald and his wife cried,

"One, two, three, *heave*!"

And the tractor went

Squelch! *Slurp*! *Splodge*!

and rolled out of the mud at last.

Just at that second, the rain stopped and a beautiful rainbow filled the sky.

"You can't beat good teamwork," beamed Old MacDonald.

"Or hens!" clucked Jenny, proudly.

Old MacDonald had a farm,

E-I-E-I-O!
And on that farm he had a tractor,
E-I-E-I-O!
With a brum, brum here
And a brum, brum there.
Here a brum,
There a brum,
Everywhere a brum, brum!
Old MacDonald had a farm,
E-I-E-I-O!

Old MacDonald had a farm, and on that farm he had some DUCKS...

Come on, Doris! *Come on,* Debbie! Don't squabble, Dora! I know you are all friends, so why do you have to quack and squawk at each other all day? You know, I can't think of a single time when you were all quiet at once. No, wait a minute, that's not right. I remember one very cold winter...

No dabbling!

On Old MacDonald's farm, there was one group of animals that caused more trouble than any other – the DUCKS! When they weren't waddling around, sticking their beaks in where they weren't wanted, they were quacking and flapping on the pond. They squabbled over slimy snails. They fought over quick little fish. They even disagreed over delicious duckweed.

"I'm so glad I'm not a duck," said Henrietta the hen to her friend Jenny, one very noisy morning. "They are *so* loud!"

"And, my dear," replied Jenny, "just imagine being wet and cold all day. I would hate it!"

"*They* seem to enjoy it," clucked Henrietta. "I suppose it's good we're all different."

167

168

But, the very next day, the hens woke up to a farm that seemed strange and different.

Henrietta poked her beak out from the hen house into the cold, frosty morning air. She couldn't work out what it was exactly, but something was definitely wrong!

Percy the pig snuffled his snout. He was puzzled, too. Something was missing? He called to Old George the horse, who was shuffling in the straw of his nice, warm stable. "George, something strange is going on."

"Something strange?" said Old George. "No, everything seems fine to me, Percy, my friend." And Percy, remembering that Old George was becoming hard of hearing, suddenly realised what it was – there was no sound from the duck pond!

It only took a few minutes for the news to spread round the barnyard. Shivering in the crisp, cold air, the animals rushed over to the pond to see what was wrong.

It was a sad sight. The pond was a solid sheet of ice. Huddled around it, looking very miserable, were the ducks.

There would be no splashing, no diving and no dabbling for the ducks that day. Without water, the ducks were still and sad.

"I never liked the squabbling," whispered Percy to Jenny, "but this is awful."

"I know what you mean," replied the hen. "A place can be *too* quiet!"

171

"We must help them," said Percy. "I can think of only one place where the water won't be frozen, but they'll have to be very, very quiet."

So, with Percy in the lead, a long line of miserable ducks waddled across the yard, into Old MacDonald's farmhouse and up the stairs to the bathroom.

Old MacDonald had just had a bath, and the water was still in the tub – warm and inviting. As the ducks dived in, they quacked and squawked in delight.

Downstairs, Old MacDonald was eating his breakfast when the happy quacking began. He looked up to the ceiling in surprise. But outside in the yard, the animals were glad things were back to normal!

Did you know?

Did you know ducks like to dance?
Their pirouettes are grand.
And what is more,
They can perform
On water or on land.

Did you know ducks like to dance?
Their leaping makes no noise.
And what is more,
They can perform
With tons and tons of poise.

Did you know ducks like to dance?
They shimmy and they shake.
And what is more,
They can perform
A very fine Swan Lake!

"There's a monster!"

There are few secrets on Old MacDonald's farm – the hens tell the pigs everything. The cows lean over the hedge to gossip to the horses, and Bruce the sheepdog keeps the sheep well informed.

But there is one place on the farm that only the ducks know about – it is down at the very bottom of the pond, where the water is cloudy.

The other animals never think about what is down there. But all that changed one spring morning when Doris the duck came quacking through the yard, her wings flapping wildly.

"There's something funny in our duck pond!" she cried.

"Calm down, Doris," said Henrietta the hen. "What on earth do you mean?"

"Down at the bottom of the pond," quacked Doris, "where it's dark and full of slithery things, there's a monster! It's got a big eye and shiny scales. What are we going to do?"

"It's probably something that's been there a long time," said Maria the sheep, who was passing by. "And just because it has shiny scales doesn't mean it's a monster!"

"It might!" said Doris. "It wasn't there yesterday. I know the bottom of that pond like I know the back of my wing. It definitely arrived in the night and it looks very, very strange."

179

When the animals arrived at the duck pond, Old MacDonald was already there. He was wearing his wading boots and climbing slowly into the water.

"Horrible," he muttered. "Why do people think they can come and dump their trash in my pond. I saw them from my window last night. Now then, what have we here?" He bent down and felt below the water.

Doris and the other ducks hid their heads under their wings, scared of what they might see. But Old MacDonald pulled out – an old television set dripping with duckweed!

Henrietta the hen collapsed with laughter, but the ducks didn't care. They would rather be laughed at by the other animals than have monsters living in their pond!

181

Where are you?

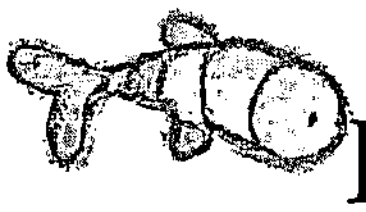

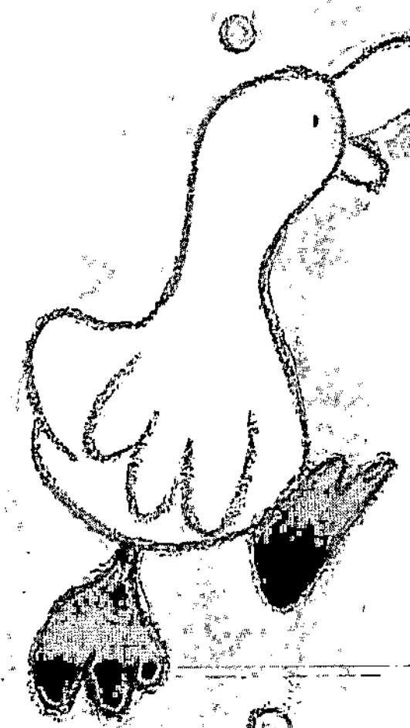

Doris Duck, Doris Duck,
Where are you?
Here I am! Here I am!
Dabbling in the dew.

Debbie Duck, Debbie Duck,
Where are you?
Here I am, catching fish.
Come and catch some too!

Dora Duck, Dora Duck,
Where are you?
Here I am, diving down,
Which I love to do!

Ducklings all, ducklings all,
Where are you?
Here we are, swimming round,
Coming to splash YOU!

184

Tails up!

The time had come for Doris the duck to teach her ducklings to dive.

"All you have to do, darlings," she quacked, "is to bob your head under the water and put your tails in the air. Just remember that –heads down, tails up!"

The ducklings nodded excitedly and had a go. (A few managed it first time.)

"Oooh!" squeaked one. "There are a lot of interesting things down there!"

"Exactly!" cried Doris. "And that is why you should learn to dive. Only ducks know what happens *under* the water."

All afternoon, the ducklings practised. Heads down! Tails up! One by one, they got the hang of it.

"Oh, Mommy, look! There are little fishes flashing about under here!" squealed one.

"There's an old pail, too!" called another.

"I've found a squiggly thing," quacked a third, "and it tastes *lovely*!"

By dinner time, all the ducklings could dive except for one.

"What's the matter, Dylan?" asked Doris.

"I'm afraid if I go down, I might not come up again," whispered the little duckling.

"But, darling," quacked Doris, "to pop right up again, all you have to do is put your head up and your tail down!"

Dylan still didn't want to try. Doris was as encouraging as she could be, but, when the sun began to set, even she was becoming a little bit impatient.

"All ducks dive, Dylan," she said. "You just have to do it. Go on!
One, two, **three**, *DIVE*!"

But Dylan still hesitated. "There *must* be some ducks who don't dive," he said. "I'm going to be one of those. I can't see the point. I'm not sure I want to catch lots of squiggly things, even if they do taste nice!"

Doris shut her beak before saying something she would regret. Then she had an idea…

"Dinner time!" announced Doris. All the little ducklings bobbed their heads up.

"We're not hungry!" they called. "We've been eating fishes and squiggly things and delicious duckweed all day."

"I haven't," said Dylan. "I'm *starving*."

So Doris dived down and found a nice fish.

"Here you are, Dylan," she quacked. "Oops!"

As Doris spoke, the fish dropped out her beak and disappeared into the water.

"My supper!" cried Dylan. Down went his head! Up went his tail! And he quickly dived down and caught his dinner.

"I did it!" he cried, bobbing up again.

"Well done!" laughed Doris, happily. "But don't talk with your mouth full, dear!"

190

Old MacDonald had a farm,

E-I-E-I-O!

And on that farm he had some ducks,

E-I-E-I-O!

With a quack, quack here

And a quack, quack there.

Here a quack,

There a quack,

Everywhere a quack, quack!

Old MacDonald had a farm,

E-I-E-I-O!

193

Old MacDonald had a farm, and on that farm he had some PIGS...

Have you ever tried to catch a piglet?
Well, don't even think about it!
Thank goodness for good old Percy here,
who's a lot older and a lot more smart,
most of the time! (He has been known to steal
my lunch from right under my nose.)
But, I wouldn't be without my pigs for
anything. Read on to find out why.

pickle the pig!

Old MacDonald has a lot of pigs on his farm.
He has two favourites – Percy, and the eldest
one, Jonathan Jakes Jermington Jollop.

Jonathan Jakes Jermington Jollop is the pig's
name, but he is called something much
shorter now! This is the story of how he got
his new name.

When Jonathan Jakes Jermington Jollop was
a piglet, he figured he was much better than
all the other animals on the farm. It was
partly because he had such a long name, and
partly because Old MacDonald liked to come
and talk with him.

"I don't know what's the matter with that young pig," clucked Henrietta the hen. "I said hello to him this morning, and he didn't say a word. He just put his nose in the air and trotted off."

"He did the same to me," neighed Old George the horse.

Soon, there wasn't an animal left on the farm who had a good word to say about Jonathan Jakes Jermington Jollop – the piglet only had himself to blame!

And that is why, when he climbed on to the roof of his sty one day, no one tried to stop him.

Jonathan Jakes Jermington Jollop saw Henry the rooster standing on top of the hen house roof, and he decided that he must try it.

Now, pigs are not well-known for their climbing skills, but this didn't stop Jonathan Jakes Jermington Jollop! He scrabbled and scrambled, puffed and panted, and eventually the young pig found himself perched uncomfortably on the very top of his sty.

It didn't take long for him to realize he had a very big problem. Getting up had not been that easy, but he could see that getting down was going to be impossible – and he suddenly knew he was scared of heights!

Soon, a crowd gathered around the pig sty. There was mooing and baaing, neighing and clucking as the other animals looked at the panicking pig on the roof.

"How did that piglet get into such a pickle – such a *mess*?" mooed Annabel.

"Hey, Pickle Piglet!" quacked Doris the duck. "What on earth are you doing up there?"

"I've been silly," said Jonathan Jakes Jermington Jollop. *"Please* get me down!"

With a laugh, Old George picked the piglet up by his tail and plonked him on the floor.

Jonathan Jakes Jermington Jollop never put on airs and graces again, and the others never let him forget his climbing adventure. And from that day on, Jonathan Jakes Jermington Jollop was forever known as *Pickles* the pig!

Watch out!

When Percy the pig feels hungry,
    There's very little doubt,
  That he will gobble anything,
      Animals, watch out!

        He nibbles straw
        At the stable door.

      He chomps on weed
    Where the ducklings feed.

      He munches hay
    When the cows are away.

      He snacks on corn
      If a sack is torn.

  When Percy the pig feels hungry,
      There's very little doubt,
    That even Old MacDonald,
  Shouldn't leave his lunch about!

Apple
Tree
Cottage

Pigs will be pigs

Everyone on Old MacDonald's farm knew that it was almost time for Old George's birthday. The horse had reached a great age – most of the animals couldn't even count that high!

"We must do something special," whispered Maria the sheep, so that George didn't hear. "We should have a party with games!"

"That might be fun for us," said Poppy the cow, "but George is a very old horse. I don't think he'd like it much."

A pig's mind is never far from food, so it was not surprising when Percy suggested that they have a feast! "If we all keep some of our food back each day, we'll have lots saved up by George's birthday!" he said.

207

Everyone agreed that a feast was a good idea. The animals found a secret place at the back of the barn to hide the party food – away from Old MacDonald's prying eyes!

Soon, they had a huge pile of the most tasty, delicious and scrummy things ready for the party – and they were all getting very excited as the day drew nearer.

The evening before the feast, the pile of food was massive! The animals knew that Mr. and Mrs. MacDonald would go to market bright and early the next morning — they would have the whole barnyard all to themselves.

As night fell, some of the little animals were almost too excited to sleep.

The moon rose over Old MacDonald's farm, and Percy was wide awake. He tossed and turned, and turned and tossed, trying hard not to think about the piles and piles of delicious food.

But, there is nothing that makes a pig so hungry as knowing there is something good to eat nearby. Though he knew that the food was meant for the party, Percy could *not* put that food out of his mind.

"Just a mouthful or two won't matter," he said to himself. "No one will miss one juicy apple, or a handful of delicious corn, will they? It won't make that much difference, will it?" Percy's mouth began to water.

Percy crept out of his sty, walking on trotter tiptoes, so he didn't make a sound. He reached the door of the barn. Creeeaaaaaak! He pushed it open with his nose and went inside.

"GOT YOU, PERCY PIG!" clucked Jenny the hen, jumping up from behind a bale of straw. "Percy, old thing," she grinned, "we knew you wouldn't be able to resist all this gorgeous food, so we've been keeping guard all week. You go straight back to bed and wait until morning." Percy couldn't help blushing. He had been caught out!

The next morning, as all the animals tucked in to the fabulous feast, Percy told the others that he was sorry.

"Don't worry," they said. "Pigs will be pigs! Have another apple, Percy!"

213

Back to the farm

Old MacDonald went to town,
Three pigs under his arm.
One didn't want to go there,
So he ran back to the farm.

Old MacDonald went to town,
Two pigs under his arm.
One kicked the farmer on his knee,
And ran back to the farm.

Old MacDonald went to town,
One pig under his arm.
He bit the farmer on the nose,
Then ran back to the farm.

The piglets didn't want to go.
They said, "We like it here!"
MacDonald said, "Okay then!"
And the pigs began to cheer!

Small and pink

One morning, Percy the pig strutted proudly through the barnyard. "Today's the day," he told everyone he passed.

"What does he mean?" said Doris the duck.

"Percy is expecting some piglets," clucked Jenny the hen. "He's very excited about it."

"I thought boy pigs couldn't have babies," said Doris, looking puzzled.

"No, no," Jenny clucked, flapping her wings. "They are coming from another farm to live with him and be part of his family."

Doris smiled. "Like Tilly and George and their new foal?" she said. "Oh, how lovely."

Percy had been waiting a long time. He had tripped and trotted from one end of the barnyard to the other more times than he liked to remember, but Old MacDonald *still* hadn't returned with the new arrivals.

Percy went back to his sty and checked it one more time. It was spotless. The straw was piled up neatly along one wall and the water trough was clean and full.

"Everything must be ready for my piglets," said Percy, brushing a speck of dust from the doorway.

Just then, he heard Old MacDonald's truck rumbling into the barnyard–they were here at last!

Percy hurried from his sty, but before he could reach the truck...

Whoosh! Something small and pink and very fast shot past his nose.

Whizzz! Something just as small and pink and even faster scuttled under his tail.

220

Wheeeee! Another small and pink and noisy thing zoomed under Percy's tummy.

"What's going on?" gasped Percy, as he spun around on his trotters.

"Eeeeeeeeee!" shrieked seven little piglets as they ran about the barnyard.

222

Late that night, a very tired Percy stood at the doorway of his sty—it was a mess. The straw was everywhere and the water trough was turned upside down. But seven little piglets were sleeping soundly in the corner.

"Tired, Percy?" asked Jenny the hen.

"Yes," sighed Percy.

"They never stand still from morning till night, do they?" added Maria the sheep.

"No," sighed Percy.

"Having second thoughts, Percy, my friend?" asked Old George the horse.

But Percy gave the kind of grin that only a very happy and contented proud pig can give. "Shhhhhhh!" he whispered. "My babies are sleeping!"

Old MacDonald had a farm,

E-I-E-I-O!

And on that farm he had some pigs,

E-I-E-I-O!

With an oink, oink here

And an oink, oink there.

Here an oink,

There an oink,

Everywhere an oink, oink!

Old MacDonald had a farm,

E-I-E-I-O!

224

225

Old MacDonald had a farm, and on that farm he had some PETS...

I love Bruce my sheepdog and my cats, Milly and Lazy. They are my pets, but like everyone else on the farm, they have work to do, too. Bruce takes care of the sheep, and the cats are supposed to take care of the mice. But, as you'll see in these stories, things don't always go to plan!

Slow down, Bruce

On Old MacDonald's farm, no one works harder than Bruce the sheepdog – except, of course, Old MacDonald! All day, Bruce races around the farm, keeping an eye on everything that goes on.

It was Bruce who barked to warn the farmer when a branch of the old apple tree was about to fall on his head!

It was Bruce who found the lambs about to escape through a hole in the hedge!

And it was Bruce who pulled one of Milly's kittens out of the duck pond.

Bruce is busy from dawn to dusk – he really loves his job!

Bruce

So, when Bruce stayed in his kennel one morning with his head on his paws, everyone began to worry.

"It's not like him," clucked Henrietta the hen.

"He can hardly open his eyes," purred Milly the cat.

"I've never seen him sick," said Old George the horse, shaking his head, "and I remember him as a pup."

Old MacDonald was more worried than any of them.

"Just stay there, old boy," he said gently. "I'll get someone to help you." And he hurried off to call the vet.

The vet arrived in record time. She had known Bruce all his life, too, and was very fond of him.

She examined him carefully, lifting his paws one by one, and checking every part of him thoroughly. Then she patted the old dog's head and said, "You're like your master. You need to stop rushing around so much and take better care of yourself. You'll be fine in a day or two, but just slow down, Bruce. Try taking it easy for once."

Bruce nodded his head gratefully and went back to sleep.

Mrs. MacDonald who was listening, returned to the farmhouse with a thoughtful look on her face.

Bruce did what he was told and by the end of the week, he was as good as new. It would soon be time to go back to work.

When he saw Old MacDonald rushing through the yard, hurrying to finish a job, Bruce raced after him.

But Mrs. MacDonald rushed out of the farmhouse and called the farmer.

"Husband!" she cried. "Did you hear what the vet said about Bruce? How can he take it easy if you don't set him a good example? Please be more thoughtful!"

So, Old MacDonald began to slow down, and Bruce did, too. The sheepdog soon felt better for it, and, strangely enough, so did Old MacDonald. And Mrs. MacDonald, who had been begging her husband to take it easy for years, felt happy.

Kittens are cuddly

Kittens are cuddly.
Kittens are sweet.
They race round the barnyard,
On soft, furry feet.
They don't stop to hear
What their mothers advise.
When trouble comes,
It is not a surprise!

They climb to the tops
Of very tall trees.
Call loudly for help
With pitiful pleas.
They chase after ducklings,
And don't stop to think.
They fall in the duck pond,
And have too much to drink!

236

It is lucky that Bruce
Quickly responds,
And helps kittens from trees
Or drags them from ponds.
And before very long,
They are kittens no more,
But cats who do nothing,
But stretch out and snore!

The new cat...

The cats on Old MacDonald's farm like nothing better than dozing. Milly loves to laze in the sun, and Lazy, like his name, hardly ever has his eyes open!

One day, Milly was snoozing on a bale of hay, when she heard Old MacDonald talking on the telephone through the open kitchen window. Half-asleep, she heard him say, "The new *cat*..." Milly was sleepy. "Yes," continued Old MacDonald, "as soon as possible. I need it – the ones I have now are *useless*."

Milly yawned and stretched for a few more minutes, still drowsy and happy. Then she suddenly sat bolt upright.What? The cats were useless? A new one was coming?

Milly raced across the barnyard to Lazy, who was fast asleep, and tried to wake him up! It wasn't easy, but she managed it at last! She repeated what she had heard at the top of her voice.

"But what's the matter with us?" yawned Lazy in a hurt voice. "I don't understand."

"You don't do anything," clucked Henrietta the hen, who was passing by (and liked to put her beak into everybody's business). "You just *sleep* all day."

Milly and Lazy looked at each other. They knew there was only one thing to do. Ten seconds later, they were tearing round the barnyard, trying to look as busy as possible!

241

By the end of a week of rushing around all day and miaowing all night, the cats had created a stir in the barnyard.

"Look here," said Bruce the sheepdog. "What exactly are you two doing? What has got into you both?"

Milly and Lazy explained. Bruce tried to hide a smile. "Well, you're doing the right thing," he barked. "You keep impressing Old MacDonald like this and you'll be fine. But I would stop the caterwauling at night, if I were you."

Bruce strolled off chuckling to himself. As Old MacDonald's right-hand dog, he knew that the farmer was waiting for a new *CAT–alogue* to order his winter boots from. But he didn't think he needed to tell Milly and Lazy that – not quite yet anyway!

Without a growl

When Old MacDonald's work is hard,
  The animals in the busy barnyard,
    Just shake their heads and sigh.
  But Bruce runs up and tries to help,
    Without a growl, a bark, or yelp,
        Or stopping to ask why.

When Old MacDonald's work is done,
  And dusk falls with the setting sun,
      He sits down in his chair.
  For he knows that he has a friend,
  From day's beginning to day's end,
    Bruce the sheepdog is there.

The perfect place

One sunny day, Old MacDonald looked out at his farm. Everything looked perfect.

But down in the barnyard, the happy scene was about to change. It was Percy the pig who noticed it first. As he lay snoozing after a good dinner of apple cores and potato peelings, he heard a little scritch-scratching in the corner of his sty. For a while, he took no notice. He was too full to move.

But the scritch-scratching went on… and on… and on… and on… until finally, Percy dragged himself up and went to see what it was.

To his surprise, he saw that a family of mice had made their home in his sty!

Meanwhile, in another corner of the busy barnyard, Old George the horse felt something tickling the back of his neck.

"Something's tickling my neck, dear," he said to Tilly, who was standing next to him in the stable. Tilly swung her big head around and peered closely at him. Then she gave a neigh of surprise!

"Why, George! There's a baby mouse asleep in your mane!"

Down by the duck pond, Doris the duck swam over to her nest. It was time to settle down in the shade for a little snooze. But she let out an angry quack when she reached the bank. Inside her nest, three little mice were playing leapfrog (or leap-mouse, I suppose)!

By the end of the day, every animal on Old MacDonald's farm had found a mouse and they were not happy! Henrietta the hen called an emergency meeting in the barnyard. No one stayed away.

"Something has to be done!" said Maria the sheep.

"Baa! Moo! Cluck! Quack! Woof! Neigh! Oink!" All the animals agreed with her. Slowly, they turned their heads and looked at Milly and Lazy, the cats.

"Keeping mice away is *your* job," said Bruce the sheepdog. "Cats eat mice!"

Lazy and Milly looked at each other. "We don't!" they said.

251

It was clear the cats were rather fond of mice – far too fond to dream of having them for dinner! None of the animals could believe their ears!

"*We're doomed*." Percy groaned.

Suddenly, above the babble, a little voice could be heard. "I'm Maisie Mouse," it squeaked. "We don't want to cause trouble, but my family has nowhere to live!"

Bruce the sheepdog had an idea. "Come with me," he said. "I know the perfect place for you. But you must be *very* quiet."

Silently, he led the mice across the yard to the farmhouse, up the stairs and into the attic.

Old MacDonald and his wife work so hard on their farm, they always sleep soundly. And that is a good thing, now that a family of mice have moved in upstairs!

253

Old MacDonald had a farm,

E-I-E-I-O!

And on that farm he had some pets,

E-I-E-I-O!

With a miaow, miaow here

And a woof, woof there.

Here a miaow,

There a woof,

Everywhere a miaow, woof!

Old MacDonald had a farm,

E-I-E-I-O!

Love to spare

Old MacDonald loves his farm,
And all the creatures there.
For though he's old,
His heart's pure gold,
With lots of love to spare.

OLD MACDONALD'S
FARM